LISA DENNIS

MAC & LAUREN ™

FLAG FUN!

INDIANAPOLIS
RACE CIRCUIT

USA

Circuit Length:
2.5 miles (4.023km)

POCKET
BOOKS

An imprint of Simon & Schuster UK Ltd. Africa House, 64-78 Kingsway, London WC2B 6AH
A Viacom Company
First published in Great Britain by Simon & Schuster UK Ltd, 2002
This paperback edition published in 2003 by Pocket Books
A CIP catalogue record for this book is available from the British Library
ISBN 0 743 46239 4
1 3 5 7 9 10 8 6 4 2

D0487000

There was quite a commotion in the pits at America's world-famous Indianapolis Motor Speedway. Mac and Lauren and their friendly racing rivals were gathered round to watch Racy Roxy testing her partner, Lucky, on his flags.

'We're here to race,' groaned Lucky. 'Who wants to do schoolwork!?'

'Computer says that to be safe on the track, you need to learn what the flags mean,' Roxy reminded him.

'So...' she went on. 'What does green mean?'

'Grass on the track!' laughed Franco.

'That's easy peasy,' revved Lucky, ignoring him. It's my favourite and it means **go!**'

'Good. How about the yellow flag with red stripes?' joined in Lauren.

'Er... Stripey bees on the loose?' guessed Lucky.

'Sorry, Lucky old boy!' laughed Wills. 'It means danger ahead on the track. You don't ever see the marshals waving it because it's normally **you** leaking oil for the rest of **us** to slip on!'

'At least you never get this flag,' added Charlie Chopper, waving it from his winch hook. 'Bruno usually gets that – for unsporting behaviour!'

Lucky closed his eyes and concentrated. 'So black and yellow means, er, oily sports... red and green means... er...'

Mac could see that Lucky was getting confused. 'Don't worry, it'll all come back to you during the race,' he said.

'Yes, come on Lucky,' Lauren said kindly. 'Let's go and find the American flag, with its stars and stripes, at the start of the race.'

'Time to go racing!' roared Mac. He led the cars to the grid.

During the warm-up lap before the race began, bullying Bruno teased Lucky. 'You won't need to know what the chequered flag means – you'll never finish the race if **I** have anything to do with it!'

'Yeah, just remember the **blue** flag, Lucky,' sneered Mad Maddy. 'It means we're faster and you have to get out of our way!'

Bruno knew all of the flags. He planned to use them to win the race...

Bruno's cousin Dash was a naughty American racing car. He didn't really like the Grand Prix cars racing on his track. So, when Bruno asked him to help ruin the race for everyone else, Dash sniggered nastily.

'I'll swap the flags around at the marshals' station!' Dash told Bruno.

'Even better, steal all the black flags,' growled Bruno. 'Then they can't send me out of the race for cheating!'

RACE POSITIONS ▲

☾	0.45.01
☽	+0.65
∿	+0.72
♥	+0.74
Ⅳ	+0.79
⋙	+0.81

The roar of the engines fought with the cheers of the crowds as the lights went out to signal the start of the race.

Round and round the cars went at dizzying speeds, with Mac and Lauren leading the way. Then, around the next bend, they saw the red-and-yellow flag. 'Slow down, Lauren,' warned Mac. 'It must be dangerous.'

But just as they carefully slowed down, Bruno and Maddy flew past. 'Ha! We tricked you with a fake flag!' laughed Bruno. 'There isn't anything wrong with the track!'

Further down the track, Wills and Harry with a screech of brakes, almost bumped into Franco and Marco. 'Fake flags?' roared Wills. 'That Bruno's a bounder!'

'We won't be fooled again!' Franco vowed.

The only car not tricked by the flag was Lucky. He'd forgotten what it meant! 'Maybe that's the "go faster" flag!' he thought. Soon he was trailing Bruno and Maddy in third place.

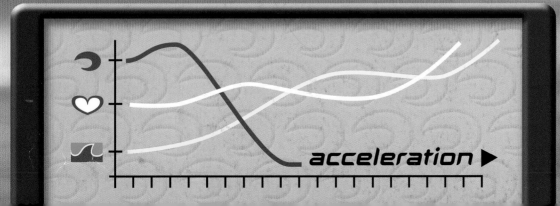

acceleration ▶

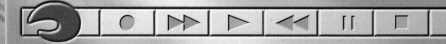

Five laps later the yellow flag warned no overtaking. 'It's another trick!' roared Wills as he sped past Mac and Lauren.

'Not this time!' shouted Lauren, but it was too late.

Mad Maddy had lost control on the bend and was spinning round and round. One of her tyres flew off in Wills's direction. Wills tried to swerve, and bumped into Roxy, pushing her into the gravel.

'I thought Lucky was the one who didn't know his flags,' teased Christian Crane as he lifted the cars to safety.

Lucky was trying to get past Bruno. But the bullying car swerved about so Lucky couldn't overtake. **Screeeeech!**

'You can't do that!' roared Lucky as he skidded dangerously close to the wall.

'With no black flag to wave, who can stop me?' thundered Bruno.

Computer could see what was happening. He radioed Mac with a special plan. 'Mac, you must find the black flag to stop Bruno and save Lucky,' said Computer. 'We think it's hidden on part of the old Brick Yard track where the Grand Prix cars aren't allowed.'

'OK, Computer,' said Mac. 'But how do I get there?'

'Our fans in the grandstand could point their flags towards the entrance!' said Lauren. A huge cheer rose up from the crowd.

Mac followed the flags and found the way through the barriers. He soon found Dash, hiding with the flags!

'Get off my track, Mac,' growled Dash. 'Or I'll bump you into the barriers!'

'I've found the flags,' Mac radioed Computer. 'But I'll need Charlie's help to get them.'

'Race control to Charlie Chopper,' Computer signalled. 'Mac needs your help on the old track!'

'On my way!' replied Charlie, and he swooped down over a surprised Dash. 'We'll soon have this problem wrapped up!'

His spinning rotors swept up the flags — and blew them over Dash so he couldn't see!

'Zoom back and finish the race, Mac,' Charlie told him. He used his winch to lift Dash in the air. 'I'll take the flags back to the finish line!'

Mac whizzed round to rejoin the race. Bruno was well in the lead. Everyone else had slowed right down because of all the fake flags flying around.

But as Charlie hovered over the finish line, Dash struggled to get away. Wrapped up in the black flag he looked like a big wrecking ball!

The marshals waved a warning flag, but Bruno ignored it. 'You can't fool me!' he roared. 'It's a trick!'

'Look out!' bellowed Dash as he flew off the winch hook and crashed into Bruno, sending them both flying out of the circuit. The crowd cheered as the two scoundrels landed in a big heap.

'I think it's time to end the race, Charlie!' radioed Computer. 'Wave the chequered flag!'

'Sure thing,' answered Charlie proudly, as Lauren and Mac zoomed past the finish line to take first and second place.

'I know what that flag means!' grinned Lucky, slowing down happily to take third place.

'Well raced, Lucky!' said Roxy proudly.

'I've seen so many flags today, I'll never forget any of them again!' laughed Lucky.

Mac and Lauren led a round of cheers. Lucky wasn't confused at all when he saw his team's flag on the podium.